Rumpelstiltskin

Barrie Wade and Neil Chapman

W
FRANKLIN WATTS
LONDON•SYDNEY

One day, long ago, the King went riding past the old mill. The foolish miller pointed to his daughter. "This girl can spin straw into gold," he said proudly.

The King took the miller's daughter to his palace and locked her in a room full of straw.

"Spin this straw into gold by morning, my girl,"
he ordered.

Of course, the poor girl didn't know how, so she wept bitterly.

Suddenly, in a flash, a strange little man appeared.

"If you give me that heart necklace,
I will spin all the straw into gold
for you."

And he did!

The next night the greedy King locked
the poor girl into a much bigger room
piled up with straw.

Again she wept floods of tears.

And again the little man appeared,
scrambling out of the straw.

"If you give me that insect ring, I will spin all this straw into gold for you. You know I can do it."

The little man
worked hard all
night – but he did it!

11

On the third night the King locked the miller's daughter into a really huge room full of towering heaps of straw.

"Spin all this straw into gold by morning," he said. "If you can do that, I shall make you my queen."

Again she wept and again the strange little man appeared. Her tears fell faster. "I have nothing left to give you," she sobbed.

"Well, I will spin the straw, if you promise to give me your first child, after you marry the King," said the little man. So the girl made her terrible promise.

The King married the miller's daughter and so made her a queen. A year later they had a beautiful child.

Soon after, the little man appeared.

"I have come for your child," he said.

"Remember your promise, Queen."

"No, I can't!" wept the Queen, shedding bitter tears.

"Sorry, but a promise is a promise," said the little man. "I will give you a chance, though," he added, craftily. "If you can guess my name in three days, then I will let you keep your child."

The Queen sent messengers to find all the names in the world – even unusual ones.

She tried many names on the first day,
but the little man said "No!" to
each one.

On the second day, the Queen read out names from a long, long list. But the little man said "No!" to every one of them.

That night, one of the Queen's messengers saw a strange little man singing and dancing by a fire in the woods.

The little man sang happily:

"The Queen won't win

the guessing game,

for RUMPELSTILTSKIN

is my name!"

On the third day when the little man
appeared, he gave the Queen a cheeky
smile. He was sure he had won.

Then the Queen said, smiling back,

"Hello, Rumpelstiltskin!"

First, the little man was astonished.

Then he grew angry, then furious.

He stamped his foot so hard that

he went right through the floor.

He was never ever seen again.

About the story

The *Rumpelstiltskin* story comes from Germany, although there are variations of the tale to be found in places as far apart as Russia and South America.

The Brothers Grimm included it in their collection of fairytales in 1812. In their tale, the King threatens to kill the miller's daughter by chopping off her head if she cannot spin the straw into gold.

Be in the story!

Imagine you are the
miller's daughter
when the King has
locked you into a
room for the third time.
Do you want to marry him?

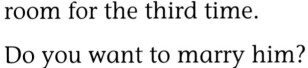

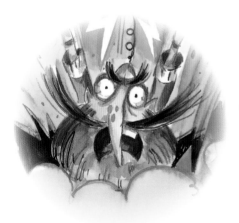

Imagine you are
Rumpelstiltskin – do
you think the Queen
has been fair at the
guessing game?

First published in 2014 by
Franklin Watts
338 Euston Road
London
NW1 3BH

Franklin Watts Australia
Level 17/207 Kent Street
Sydney
NSW 2000

A CIP catalogue record for this book is available
from the British Library.

The artwork for this story first appeared in
Leapfrog: Rumpelstiltskin

ISBN 978 1 4451 2863 4 (hbk)
ISBN 978 1 4451 2864 1 (pbk)
ISBN 978 1 4451 2866 5 (library ebook)
ISBN 978 1 4451 2865 8 (ebook)

Series Editor: Jackie Hamley
Series Advisor: Catherine Glavina
Series Designer: Cathryn Gilbert

Printed in China

Franklin Watts is a divison of
Hachette Children's Books,
an Hachette UK company.
www.hachette.co.uk